DISCARD

CHESTERFIELD COUNTY PUBLIC LIBRARY
CHESTERFIELD, VA

DISCARD

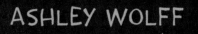

ASHLEY WOLFF

WHERE,
oh where, is baby bear?

Beach Lane Books
New York   London   Toronto   Sydney   New Delhi

One by one, bats fly out of the deep, dark den.

"Where are they going?" asks Baby Bear.

"They are going to look for food," says Mama Bear.

"Can we go look for food too?" asks Baby Bear.

"Yes," says Mama. "Let's go."

Mama Bear sniffs the warm night air.

But when she looks around,

Baby Bear is nowhere in sight.

"Where, oh where, is Baby Bear?" calls Mama.

e I am, Mama," says Baby Bear.

ide the mossy log."

Mama Bear gobbles berries.
But when she looks around,
Baby Bear is nowhere in sight.
"Where, oh where, is Baby Bear?" calls Mama.

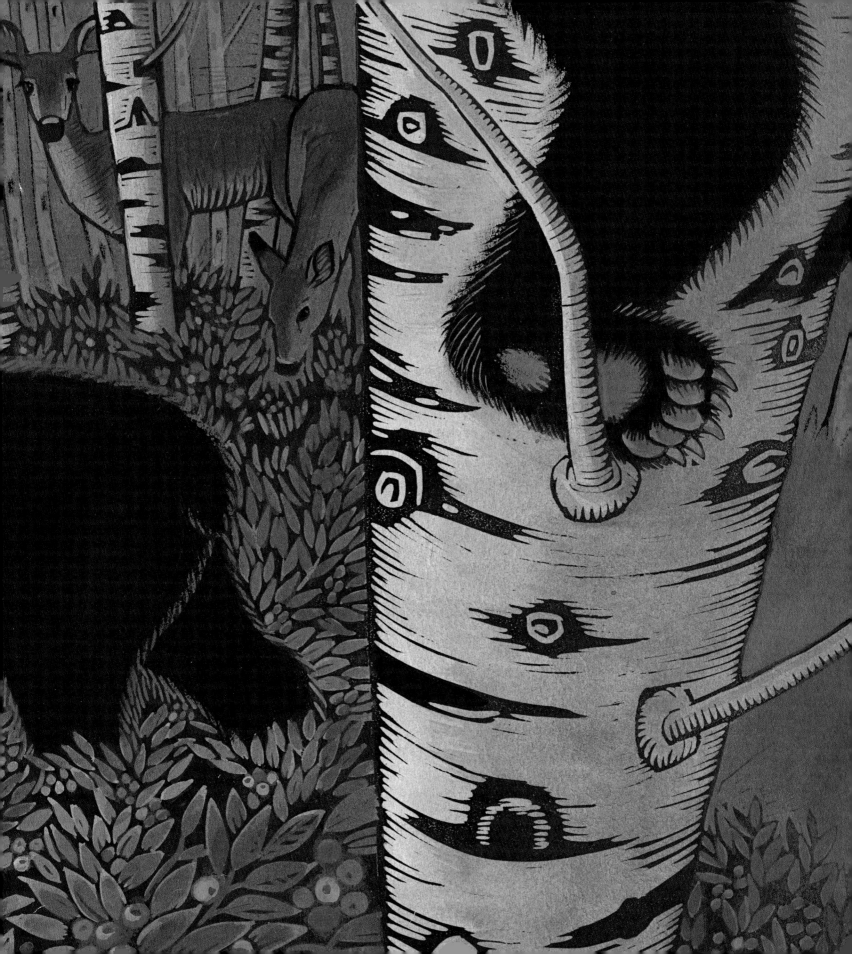

"Here I am, Mama," says Baby Bear.
"Up in the birch tree."

Mama Bear catches a wiggling trout.
But when she looks around,
Baby Bear is nowhere in sight.
"Where, oh where, is Baby Bear?" calls Mama.

"Here I am, Mama," says Baby Bear.
"Behind the waterfall."

Mama Bear laps water.
But when she looks around,
Baby Bear is nowhere in sight.
"Where, oh where, is Baby Bear?" calls Mama.

"Here I am, Mama," says Baby Bear.
"Between the cattails."

Mama Bear chews a mouthful of dandelions.
But when she looks around,
Baby Bear is nowhere in sight.
"Where, oh where, is Baby Bear?" calls Mama.

"Here I am, Mama," says Baby Bear.
"On top of the boulder."

"Come along now, Baby Bear," says Mama.

across the river,

between the birch trees,

down
the
cliff,

and into their den.

Baby Bear watches the bats
return to their roost.
"Where, oh where,
is Mama Bear?" he calls.

"Here I am, Baby Bear,"
says Mama,
"right beside you."

Where, oh where, is Oliver Martin?
In my heart, that's where!
—A. W.

BEACH LANE BOOKS
An imprint of Simon & Schuster Children's Publishing Division
1230 Avenue of the Americas, New York, New York 10020
Copyright © 2017 by Ashley Wolff
All rights reserved, including the right of reproduction in whole or in part in any form.
BEACH LANE BOOKS is a trademark of Simon & Schuster, Inc.
For information about special discounts for bulk purchases, please contact Simon &
Schuster Special Sales at 1-866-506-1949 or business@simonandschuster.com.
The Simon & Schuster Speakers Bureau can bring authors to your live event. For more
information or to book an event, contact the Simon & Schuster Speakers Bureau at
1-866-248-3049 or visit our website at www.simonspeakers.com.
Book design by Lauren Rille
The text for this book was set in Joppa.
The illustrations for this book were made by printing linoleum blocks in black on Arches
Cover paper. These are then hand-colored with watercolor.
Manufactured in China
0717 SCP
First Edition
2 4 6 8 10 9 7 5 3 1
CIP data for this book is available from the Library of Congress.
ISBN 978-1-4814-9916-3
ISBN 978-1-4814-9917-0 (eBook)